J.B. Wigglebottom
and the
Parade of Pets

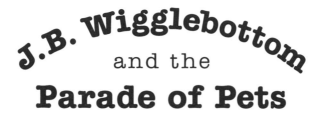

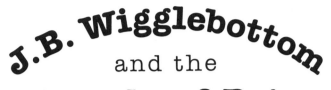

J.B. Wigglebottom
and the
Parade of Pets

by Vivian Sathre

illustrated by Catharine O'Neill

ATHENEUM   1993   NEW YORK

Maxwell Macmillan Canada
Toronto
Maxwell Macmillan International
New York   Oxford   Singapore   Sydney

Atheneum
Macmillan Publishing Company
866 Third Avenue
New York, NY 10022

Maxwell Macmillan Canada, Inc.
1200 Eglinton Avenue East
Suite 200
Don Mills, Ontario M3C 3N1

Macmillan Publishing Company is part of the Maxwell Communication Group of Companies.

First edition
Printed in the United States of America
10 9 8 7 6 5 4 3 2 1
Book design by Kimberly Adlerman

Library of Congress Cataloging-in-Publication Data
Sathre, Vivian.
J. B. Wigglebottom and the parade of pets / Vivian Sathre.
p.   cm.
Summary: Because of his little sister's allergies, J.B. doesn't have a pet to enter in his fourth grade class parade, but he has to come up with some idea to beat the bully who is always picking on him.
ISBN 0-689-31811-1
[1. Schools—Fiction.   2. Bullies—Fiction.   3. Brothers and sisters— Fiction.   4. Pets—Fiction.]   I. Title.
PZ7.S24916Jaf   1993
[Fic]—dc20   92-17375

To Roger,
for his understanding and support

Chapter 1

Jonathon Bradford Higgenbottom was better known as J. B. "Wigglebottom" to the other fifth graders at Lincoln Elementary School. J. B. didn't like the nickname. He didn't like the kid who gave it to him either: Buddy Zimmers. Buddy thought he was the greatest at everything. Sometimes he was. Sometimes he was a pain in the neck. Just once J. B. would like to show him up.

J. B. stared into his social studies book and pretended to read while his thoughts wandered home to the chocolate cupcakes his mom baked every Wednesday. His stomach growled.

Emory Harrison leaned forward and guffawed.

He slipped a piece of fudge-covered peanut butter bubble gum onto J. B.'s desk.

"Thanks," J. B. whispered. "I'm starving." It was nice having his best friend sitting right behind him. It almost made up for Buddy sitting in front of him. He glanced at the clock. Ten minutes to go, then he could hurry home and stuff his face with cupcakes.

As J. B. was about to shove the gum into his mouth, Buddy bent down to pick up his pencil. J. B. leaned closer to his book and waited. Mrs. Rudd had too clear a view with Buddy's head out of the way. What was taking so long anyway? How could it take so long to pick up a pencil?

Finally Buddy's head popped into sight. With one quick glance to make sure Mrs. Rudd wasn't looking, J. B. shoved the gum into his mouth.

A second later Mrs. Rudd's chair scraped across the floor. She sprang to her feet and looked around. Her stare landed on J. B.

His heart raced. She must have seen him chew. Or maybe she *heard* him chew. Maybe she smelled the chocolate. He wondered if he should swallow the evidence or just get out a piece of paper and begin his "I will not chew gum in school" sentences.

Mrs. Rudd walked down the aisle toward him. Now his heart pounded in his chest *and* his ears. Once he'd asked Emory about a heart beating in two places like that, and Emory had told him it was just his heart beating faster. He still didn't understand how that gave him a heartbeat in his head. He wanted to ask his dad—his heart thudded faster and louder as Mrs. Rudd got closer—but he only remembered the double beats when he heard them, and that was usually when he was getting scolded. Scoldings were not the time to ask about your heartbeat, or anything else for that matter.

Mrs. Rudd stopped in front of his desk.

J. B. held his breath and tried not to move his jaw.

But Mrs. Rudd turned away and looked over the rest of the class. J. B. cautiously breathed again. Mrs. Rudd glanced at the clock and said, "I have some exciting news I'd like to share with you before the bell rings."

J. B. began to wiggle in his seat.

"As you know, it's almost time for summer

vacation. This is the time of year Mr. Westin, our principal, names the class he feels has exhibited the best lunchroom behavior throughout the year." Mrs. Rudd looked up as the intercom squeaked on. "I'll let Mr. Westin tell you the rest."

"Good afternoon." The principal's voice sounded muffled through the speaker. "It was a difficult decision to make, but I have once again chosen 'the Best Behaved Class in the Lunchroom.' As in the past, the winning class will have the privilege of presenting a special Parade of Pets at a special assembly on Friday." Suddenly his voice boomed. "Congratulations to Mrs. Rudd and her fifth graders!"

Cheers went up from everyone in the class. Everyone, except J. B. He groaned. The Parade of Pets. Big deal. Thanks to his little sister, Kate, he couldn't have a pet. And this was the third time the class he'd been in had won. Why did *his* sister have to be allergic to animals?

"I am very proud of you kids." Mrs. Rudd smiled. "My past classes have done well in most of Mr. Westin's competitions, but it has been six years since my class was chosen the best behaved. You deserve to give yourselves a hand." She started clapping, and soon everyone joined in.

"I want you to remember this is not *just* a parade. Over the years it has turned into a contest too." She walked around the room. "Mr. Westin loves contests! If your pet does anything special, show it off. After the parade, the teachers will vote for the entry they feel is the most unforgettable. A good trick or an unusual animal is bound to get you votes."

Buddy's hand shot up.

"Yes?" Mrs. Rudd asked.

Buddy looked directly at J. B. and grinned. "What if you don't have a *real* pet?"

Mrs. Rudd slipped her hands into her skirt pockets. "As other students have in the past, you may enter whatever you wish in the parade. Be creative. I'm sure everyone can come up with something. Your entry doesn't actually have to be a pet. One year someone brought a stuffed dinosaur that turned inside out to become a dragon. Now that's a neat trick for a stuffed animal."

The bell rang. J. B. closed his book and

shoved it into his backpack. A neat trick all right, but it wasn't neat enough to win the contest.

Ms. Nye, one of the sixth-grade teachers, poked her head in the doorway. "Congratulations, you lucky ducks!" Smiling and waving, she hurried off.

Mrs. Rudd nodded after her. "See you tomorrow, class. We'll talk more about the parade in the morning. Remember to study your spelling tonight."

J. B. slipped his backpack over one shoulder and stood up, but when he stepped forward, his foot caught. He tripped. His backpack slammed to the floor the same time he did, creating a loud *whap!*

From where he lay, it was easy to see why he fell. One of the laces from his left shoe had been tied to one of the laces from his right shoe. So that's why Buddy had taken so long to pick up his pencil. Grumbling, J. B. untied his shoes. Buddy Zimmers was at it again!

Chapter 2

Buddy elbowed J. B. as he stood up. "You're like a bull in a china shop, Wigglebottom. Yeah, that's what my mom would say." He followed J. B. down the aisle. "Speaking of bulls, what are you going to bring to the parade *this* year? I bet it'll be something stupid again."

J. B. clenched his teeth and walked faster. He filed "bull in a china shop" in the back of his mind to ask Emory about later.

As soon as J. B. stepped outside the building, Buddy purposely rammed him as he ran past. "See you, Wigglebottom."

"Good riddance," J. B. mumbled.

Emory stepped outside right behind him and

shielded his eyes from the spring sunlight. He studied a spoon for a minute, then shoved it into his back pocket.

J. B. shifted his backpack to his other shoulder and shook his head. Emory was always studying something. "Okay, Einstein, any brilliant ideas on what I can take to the parade?"

Emory smiled; J. B. knew he liked being referred to as "Einstein." He'd probably grow up to be a scientist too.

Finally Emory cocked his head. "How about another fish?"

Some of Emory's ideas weren't all that great. J. B. wished he had a llama or an alligator. But he knew he'd be just as happy with something less spectacular, like a cat, if it knew neat tricks. He kicked a rock, followed it as it bounced across the concrete, then kicked it again. "Naw. When I dropped the fishbowl on the kitchen floor, Mom said no more fish."

"That was a year ago. Maybe she's forgotten by now."

They waited at the curb with the other kids until the crossing guards led them across the street. "I don't think so, Emory. There was glass and slimy green water all over the place. It smelled worse than my sneakers." He shook his head. "She'll remember that forever. Besides, fish can't do tricks."

J. B. sighed. He wanted to bring a really neat pet to school. One better than Buddy's. But that would be impossible, even if Kate wasn't allergic to animals. Buddy's dad not only owned the biggest pet shop in town but even worked to help relocate wild animals. The ones people tried to make into pets. Last year Buddy brought a parrot to the parade. The parrot wore a little silver top hat and sang "Yankee Doodle" all the way through. With no mistakes!

Just then, Bailey, the neighbor's dog, pranced over to greet J. B. Both boys bent down to pet him before continuing on.

Bailey tried to follow them, but the rope he was tied to only let him go as far as the sidewalk. "Sorry, boy," J. B. said.

When they reached his house, J. B. cut across the lawn. "Meet me at the tree camp in five minutes. My mom made cupcakes."

"Great." Emory licked his lips, then hurried on.

J. B. stopped just outside his front door. "Wait a minute, Emory."

Emory turned and walked backward so he could see J. B.

"What's 'like a bull in a china shop' mean?"

Emory grinned. "That you're clumsy."

J. B. wrinkled his nose and walked inside. Suddenly Kate's arms were around his waist. She hugged him tight. "Hi, J. B."

"Hi, Kate," he said, looking at the top of her head as he slipped his backpack off his shoulder. "How was kindergarten today?"

"I learned five more new words. Want me to read them to you?"

"Sure."

Kate stepped back from J. B. and looked up.

"Oh no!" He pushed her away as soon as he spotted the chocolate smeared all around her mouth. He pulled at his shirt. "You got chocolate all over my Gecko shirt, and it'll probably stain. I can't just fly to Hawaii and buy a new one, you know. Sometimes you can be a real pain, Kate!"

Kate's bottom lip quivered.

Mom stood in the kitchen doorway. "She

didn't mean to do it, J. B. Put your shirt in the laundry room and I'll soak it."

J. B. thought about apologizing, then looked at his shirt again. Kate was always causing him problems. Suddenly he remembered his biggest problem had nothing to do with his shirt, but had a lot to do with Kate and her allergies. His biggest problem was the Parade of Pets on Friday. And he had less than two days to come up with a solution.

Chapter 3

After changing his shirt, J. B. chose the four biggest cupcakes and put them on a paper plate. He carefully carried them to the camp he had made under the big trees in the backyard.

Emory was there waiting for him, and he reached for a cupcake as J. B. set the plate down between them. "Two each. Yum." He offered J. B. a cookie from his shirt pocket. "Bran and bean curd. My mom made them. If I'd told her about the cupcakes, it would've hurt her feelings."

J. B. eyed the cookie and wrinkled his nose. "No thanks." Emory's mom wasn't a very good cook with regular food; he certainly didn't want

13

to chance tasting a cookie she made with weird stuff like bran and bean curd.

J. B. stuck his gum onto the back of his hand, then grabbed a cupcake. Curling his tongue, he scooped a gob of frosting into his mouth. "Mmmm." The sun winked at him between the leaves and made him squint. He thought about what Buddy had said to him about bringing something stupid to the parade.

"I hate the parade! What am I going to do for a pet? I can't buy a fish and if I bring worms again like I did in first grade, Buddy will never let me forget it."

Emory shrugged, pulled a spoon from his back pocket, and stared at it as he ate.

"Why do you keep looking at that spoon?"

Emory moved the spoon back and forth in the light. "Haven't you ever noticed that in one side you're upside down, and in the other side you're not?"

J. B. shook his head, but Emory was too busy looking at the spoon to notice.

"I think it has something to do with one side being concave and one side being convex."

J. B. licked the rest of the frosting off his

cake. "Come on, Emory. Forget the spoon. I need help." He leaned back against the tree. "Even if I could buy a fish, I'd need two hundred years to teach it a trick." He pulled the cupcake from the paper and bit into it.

Emory stuffed the spoon back in his pocket and brushed an ant off his leg. "You could take Tinker."

J. B. sat upright. "You'd do that—let me take your gerbil?"

Emory nodded. "Sure."

J. B. fell back against the tree. "Thanks, Emory, but I couldn't do that. Then you wouldn't have a pet. Everybody knows Tinker belongs to you." J. B. wanted his own pet, one better than Buddy's. A pet that could win the prize. When he looked at Emory, it was almost as if Emory had read his mind.

"Tinker can't do any tricks, so she won't win." He grabbed another cupcake and stuffed half of it into his mouth.

Darn! J. B. had been hoping Emory wouldn't want his second one. J. B. sighed. As he reached for his own second one, Kate raced up, kicking dirt across the plate and his cupcake.

15

"My sunflowers are starting to grow, J. B. Want to see them?"

J. B. picked up his cupcake and shoved it toward her. "Look what you've done!" He flipped the cupcake upside down and tapped the bottom of it. The dirt clung to the frosting. He blew on it, but still the dirt stuck to the top of the cupcake. When he tried brushing off the dirt, it ground into the frosting.

Emory pulled his legs up Indian-style. "It was an accident, J. B. She didn't mean to do it."

J. B. ignored him and glared at Kate. "You're always ruining things for me. No cupcake because of you, and no pet for the parade because of you. Why do you have to be allergic to animals? Why couldn't you be allergic to chocolate or spinach?" He folded the plate in half, smashing the dirty cupcake. "Just scram, Kate. Scram!"

As he stomped off toward the house, Kate began to cry. "I'm never going to show you anything ever again, J. B."

Who cares? he thought, shutting the door on her sobs.

He stuffed the plate into the garbage, turned

on the kitchen faucet, and sucked a drink from the stream of water. When he walked back outside, Kate was gone. He plopped down next to Emory.

Emory stuck out his hand. "What about a caterpillar?"

J. B. looked at the furry caterpillar curled up in Emory's palm. He scowled. "For the parade? Sure, Emory. I'll just tell it to turn into a butterfly at nine Friday morning."

"You sure are in a bad mood today. I was only trying to help." Emory stood up and set the caterpillar down near the trunk of a tree. "I think I'll go to the field and see if anyone's playing ball." He took a few steps, then turned back around. "Want to come?"

J. B. thought about it as he flicked ants off the cupcake papers he'd forgotten to take back into the house. One ant landed on Emory's sneaker. "Oops. Sorry." He put his face down closer to the papers. "Look at these little buggers. They like chocolate cake too. And look." He pointed. "Zillions of them are coming."

Emory leaned forward. "There must be an anthill around here somewhere." He looked at

J. B. "Are you coming to the field with me or not?"

J. B. kept flicking ants. He thought about Kate and his dirty cupcake. "I'll meet you over there. There's something I have to do first."

Chapter

4

If he was going to apologize to Kate, he needed to do it while he was still in the mood, and before she did anything else to bug him.

J. B. checked the front yard and the garage. Then he looked in Kate's room, but he couldn't find Kate. He walked into the kitchen as Mom climbed onto a chair to change a light bulb.

"Mom, have you seen Kate?"

"She came in a few minutes ago and got Bimbo. Said she was going to Tamara's house." Mom looked him in the eyes. "What's up?" She rested one hand on her hip. "You aren't picking on her, are you, J. B.? You're a lot older than she is. She's little and her feelings get hurt easily."

"I know," J. B. answered. And he knew Kate only carried her stuffed monkey around when she felt terrible, or if it was bedtime. Then it hit him. What about *his* feelings? Didn't it matter that *she* bugged him all the time? No—never, never, never. *She's* little so she gets away with murder! And didn't anybody care that he was going to look stupid in the parade again this year, just because of her?

J. B. stuffed his hands in his pockets. "May I go to the field?"

"Sure, honey," Mom answered. "But don't be late for dinner."

Yuk! He hated it when she called him "honey." It was so mushy; it was worse than being called Wigglebottom.

A moment later he pedaled away on his bike. A game of kickball was just what he needed to take his mind off his troubles. Maybe it'd even clear his head enough to come up with an idea for the parade.

At the edge of the field he skidded to a stop. Softball! "Just my luck," he muttered. He wasn't very good at any sport, but this one was his very worst.

21

On the pitcher's mound stood Buddy Zimmers. Emory stood near first base, while the Miller brothers, Rhett and Ronnie, covered second and third. Kelly-Lynn Daniels was their only outfielder, and Jeff Hukara was their catcher.

Emory waved. "Come on, J. B. You can be on our team."

"No way," Buddy said, tossing the ball into the air and then catching it. "Wigglebottom couldn't hit a *basketball* with a bat, let alone a softball."

Some of the kids snorted and giggled; Emory got a funny look on his face and stared into space.

J. B. glared at him. Why wasn't Emory sticking up for him? Maybe Emory thought he was still in a bad mood. Or maybe, he thought, Emory didn't want to be his *best* friend anymore.

Finally Buddy pointed at the other team. "You only have five players. We have six." He grinned. "He's all yours."

Jason, the next batter, moaned. "We don't need another player. Especially Wigglebottom. He *always* strikes out."

Brent, who stood waiting to bat after Jason, shielded his eyes from the sun. "Come on, you guys. Give him a chance. How's he supposed to get any better if you never let him play?" He took a step backward. "Come on, J. B. You can bat before me."

J. B. liked the way Brent stuck up for him. He jumped off his bike and trotted over to stand in front of Brent.

Buddy pitched the ball to Jason. Jason let it pass. Jeff caught it and tossed it back to Buddy.

Buddy pitched another ball. This time Jason swung, smacked the ball into the outfield, then ran to first base. Kelly-Lynn got the ball, saw that Jason was safe, and threw it back to Buddy.

Buddy grinned as J. B. stepped up to the plate. "And now, Wigglebottom the Great!"

J. B. sighed and took a practice swing. Just once he'd like to hit the ball hard enough to hear the same loud *crack!* he heard when the other guys hit it.

Buddy eyed him. "Okay, guys, get ready for Wigglebottom the Great. I bet he'll hit the ball to South America if we're not careful. Places, everyone! Keep your eyes on the ball—"

23

Jason stole second base.

"Shut up and pitch the ball!" Kelly-Lynn shouted.

J. B. tightened his grip on the bat.

"Here it comes, Wigglebottom, ready or not." Buddy threw the ball. It seemed to come at J. B. in slow motion. He swung so hard he almost spun in a circle.

Crack! His heart beat faster as he dropped the bat and ran.

The edge of the bat had connected with the ball, but had sent it slow and high instead of fast and far. His teammates groaned.

"Ooh, ooh! Here it comes," Buddy mimicked in a high, babyish voice. "Ooh, ooh! I don't know if I can catch it—it might hurt me."

J. B. hit first base, his heart pounding, just in time to see the ball drop neatly into Buddy's mitt.

Emory scratched his armpit, elbowing J. B. at the same time. "You're out, J. B."

"Brilliant deduction, Einstein!" J. B. snapped. He headed off the field. Besides having Kate and Emory mad at him, now his whole team was probably mad at him too.

Nobody else on his team struck out. Just before it was his turn to be up again, J. B. climbed on his bike. "I can't stay any longer." He wasn't going to stick around for more of Buddy's teasing. "I'm looking for Kate." It wasn't really a lie. He *had* been looking for her. "Any of you guys seen her? She's carrying a stuffed monkey." He knew they hadn't. Not unless they'd been to Tamara's house.

Buddy laughed. "What's the matter, Wigglebottom? Did your little sister steal your pet?" He rested his weight on one foot and grinned. His voice was mocking. "I bet you have another stuffed animal you could bring to the parade."

J. B.'s face grew hot. He thought about the rhyme he used to chant when he was little.

> Some words are short,
> Some words are long,
> Some words are right,
> But your words are wrong!

But that rhyme seemed too babyish now.

What J. B. really wanted was to push in

Buddy's face. Instead, he turned his bike toward home.

"Better run home and feed your pet some more stuffing," Buddy yelled after him. He laughed a taunting laugh. "I can hardly wait to see what you come up with this year!"

All the way home J. B. thought about how lousy he was in sports, how lousy Buddy was to him, and how lousy his own pets had been in the two other pet parades.

After pushing his bike into the garage, he collapsed in the shade of his tree camp. Everything seemed so unfair. Somewhere there had to be a pet better than Buddy's, whatever Buddy's pet might be. Maybe this year Buddy would bring a bird that could sing *and* dance.

J. B. tossed a pebble into the air. He stuck his hand out to catch it, but missed. He couldn't even catch a lousy pebble thrown a foot into the air! He sighed, then remembered the cupcake papers with the ants. He looked for them, but they were gone. Finally he spotted one. The wind must have moved it. He crawled closer. It was nearly black with ants. Two thin black

threads of scurrying ants led to and from the paper.

An idea popped into J. B.'s mind. He ran to the kitchen and dug through the cupboards. From underneath the sink, he pulled out an empty peanut can. Good!

J. B. rushed back to the yard. His heart beat faster. This was a great idea! His best!

With one quick scoop of his hand, J. B. pushed the ants into the can. He snapped on the lid.

Maybe now he had a chance of beating Buddy!

Kate watched J. B. as he ate dinner. He thought about apologizing for treating her so mean, but he couldn't. Not while his parents were listening. He pushed a green bean around his plate and glanced at his dad and mom from the corner of his eye. They'd ask all kinds of questions. He'd end up telling them about the Parade of Pets. Then they'd say something silly like, "A year from now this won't seem so important to you, J. B." Ha!

Kate tried to stab the last piece of meat on her plate. When she couldn't, she picked it up with her fingers and stuck it on the end of her fork. "You should see my sunflowers, Daddy. They're growing."

Dad faked surprise and exchanged glances with Mom. "Already?"

"Yep. They're this big." Kate held up her thumb and finger about a half an inch apart.

"That's wonderful, Kate. Sounds like you're taking good care of them."

"Yep. They're just babies and they need me to make sure they get water."

Dad listened and nodded while Kate jabbered on. After a while he took seconds of rice and passed the bowl on to J. B. "And how was your day today?"

"Fine." He didn't want to tell them how it really went, finding out about the parade and getting Buddy's teasing.

"Tell us one of the 'fine' things that happened." Dad shoved a heaping forkful of rice into his mouth.

J. B. couldn't think of anything *fine*, except for his ants, and he couldn't mention them without mentioning the parade. He wiggled. "One thing that happened was that after school we played baseball and I actually *hit* the ball when it was my turn to bat. The bad thing was, it was a fly ball and someone caught it." He stared at his plate. "I'm not very good."

"How about we walk over to the field after dinner and practice?"

J. B. passed the rice bowl on to Mom. "No thanks, Dad. I have a lot of homework."

"You sure?"

J. B. nodded. Right now he was more interested in the parade than baseball.

"Chocolate cupcakes for dessert," Mom said, handing one to each of them. J. B. ate his in four and a half bites. He wished he hadn't taken two cupcakes for himself at snack time so he could have another one now.

Kate ate less than half of hers and offered it to J. B. "You want this? I'm full."

"Sure, Kate. Thanks." Sometimes she was so nice. Now he felt even more cruddy for yelling at her.

J. B. shoved Kate's cupcake in his mouth, then cleared the table. He spotted an empty margarine tub setting on the counter. He held it up and looked at his mom. "May I have this? I need it for school."

Mom nodded. "Let me rinse it out first."

"That's okay. I can do it." J. B. turned on the water.

Beside the sink was the pile of dirty plates. J. B. eyed the scraps on the top plate. There were pork chop bones, kernels of rice, green beans, and a hunk of dry biscuit. J. B. dropped some of each into his tub. What if this stuff didn't work? He threw in a cupcake paper just in case.

He hurried outside and set the tub of scraps close to where the ant-covered cupcake papers had been. Then he sat down and waited for more ants to come. He waited and waited. Not one ant came. The sun was starting to go down. Just as he was about to go into the house, J. B. heard a rustling behind him.

His heart pounded. No ant could make that kind of noise.

The rustling moved closer. His heart pounded so loud it almost drowned out the rustling.

Afraid to turn around J. B. closed his eyes and took a deep breath. He'd count to three, then turn. One. Two—

"Yeow!" Something cold and slimy slithered across the back of his neck. J. B. jumped up, clawing at whatever it was on his neck.

Bailey, the neighbor's dog, yelped.

J. B. turned around. He put his hand over his thudding heart. "You scared me, Bailey!"

Bailey dropped his tail between his legs and hung his head.

J. B. started inside, stopped, and turned around. He bent down and massaged Bailey's ears, checking his nose for scratches. "I'm sorry, boy. You scared me, that's all."

When J. B. stood up, Bailey started to follow him toward the house. J. B. pointed to the yard next door. "Go on home, Bailey. You're going to get into trouble for being loose."

Bailey wagged his tail as if saying good-bye, then left.

J. B. went to his room. He thought about studying his spelling list. Instead, he pulled out his latest book of knock-knock jokes and flopped down on the bed.

He kept glancing from his watch to his alarm clock; they both showed the same time. He was sure the longer he waited, the more ants he'd catch. To beat Buddy he needed lots of ants. The thought of beating Buddy made him smile.

Just before bed he took his peanut can outside to collect the ants from the margarine tub. It wasn't quite dark, but J. B. turned on the porch light anyway.

Kate was crouched down in the corner of the yard. J. B. grinned. She was probably checking to see if her sunflowers had grown any bigger since this afternoon. He would apologize to her right after collecting his ants.

J. B. walked to the tree camp, but when he reached down for the container, it was gone! He dropped to his knees and searched.

"What are you looking for?" Kate asked, coming up behind him.

J. B. jumped at her sudden closeness. "My ant trap. Will you help . . ." Turning, he saw the plastic container in Kate's hand. "What are you doing with that?"

"Nothing." Kate sneezed and rubbed her eyes.

J. B. took a step toward her. "This is important, Kate!" He grabbed the container. It

was empty. "What did you do with the ants that were in here?"

Tears welled up in Kate's already red, puffy eyes. "Why don't you ask Bailey? He was the one who had it." She stomped off toward the house.

J. B. groaned. So that's why Bailey had been hanging around—for a snack! He'd probably eaten the missing cupcake papers too.

J. B. plopped down on the porch steps and rested his elbows on his knees. He set his chin on his hands and stared into the darkness. Instead of apologizing to Kate, he'd made things worse.

"Bedtime!" Mom called from the window.

J. B.'s mind raced. He still needed more ants. He'd have to set up another trap. "May I stay up a few more minutes?"

"Not tonight, honey. You've been up late all week."

"Oh, Mom." J. B. sighed and walked inside. Now his trap would have to wait until morning. He was beginning to wonder if his idea would really work. He doubted he would ever get to sleep tonight!

Chapter 6

His mother pounded on the bedroom door. "Get up this minute, J. B., or you're going to be late for school."

J. B. rolled over and scratched his face. Night couldn't be over yet. It seemed as if he'd just fallen asleep. And his alarm hadn't buzzed yet.

Suddenly he remembered why he couldn't get to sleep last night—he needed to get more ants. This was his only chance to be better than Buddy. He couldn't mess it up now. He sprang out of bed. Squinting at the clock on his dresser, he groaned. He'd forgotten to set his alarm last night. School started in fifteen minutes!

J. B. picked yesterday's clothes off the floor

and dressed. Then he took giant steps out to the kitchen table.

"Hurry, honey." Mom set down scrambled eggs and toast in front of him.

Honey again! Ugh. He shoveled the eggs into his mouth in three bites. As he was about to stuff in the toast he got an idea.

He glanced at Mom, then scraped the last of the strawberry jam from the jar and spread it across his toast. "I'll eat this on the way." He gulped his milk, grabbed his lunch off the counter, and got his coat and backpack from the hall closet.

J. B. ran around to the backyard. He set the toast down under the trees, took a deep breath, and squeezed his eyes shut. *Please make the ants like strawberry jam as much as they like chocolate cake.* Turning, he ran as fast as he could to school.

As J. B. hurried to his desk Buddy stuck his foot into the aisle. J. B. tripped, but caught himself before he fell. He hung his backpack on his chair and slipped his coat off.

"There's a red bug on your collar," Buddy said. "Is that your new pet?"

Without thinking, J. B. checked his collar. Buddy laughed.

There wasn't any bug. J. B. felt stupid. Sometimes he really hated the way Buddy acted. He slid into his seat as the final bell rang.

Emory poked him in the back. "Where were you this morning?" he whispered.

"I overslept."

Mrs. Rudd stood up from behind her desk. "Good morning, class. Happy Thursday." She grinned. "Are you ready to hear more about the Parade of Pets, or should we wait until later? I know you're all eager to work on our spelling and math."

"Parade of Pets," the kids answered.

Mrs. Rudd walked around her desk and half leaned, half sat on the front of it. As her skirt spread out it reminded J. B. of a flowered parachute. "Tomorrow morning, bring your pets to school with you. The assembly will start right after roll call. Some of you may need your parent's help. That's fine, they're welcome to come."

Mrs. Rudd folded her hands in her lap. "One more thing. All live pets must be on a leash or in a box so they aren't running around loose. And *please* make sure that whatever kind of container you bring, it won't scratch the gym floor. You know how particular Mr. Westin is about that floor." She took a deep breath. "Boxes are nice if your pet is small because then it's kept a surprise." She looked around. "Any questions?"

Buddy raised his hand.

"Yes?" Mrs. Rudd asked.

"Who gets to go first?"

Mrs. Rudd stood up and walked around the class. "We will show our pets in alphabetical order." She pointed to Mindy Adams. "You'll go first." She looked at Buddy. "You'll be last."

"Saving the best for last," Buddy whispered to J. B.

Show-off, J. B. thought, leaning on one elbow. But Buddy was probably right. Mrs. Rudd *was* saving the best for last.

"One final thing," Mrs. Rudd said. "The winner will be announced Friday afternoon, just before the last bell. Besides going out to lunch with the principal on Monday, the winner will also get an extra surprise this year."

"What kind of surprise?" Emory asked.

Mrs. Rudd smiled. "You'll have to wait until Friday to find that out." She headed back to her desk. "Now let's get to work. Take out your math books, please."

Some of the kids moaned, but not J. B. He thought the sooner the work got done, the faster the day would pass.

Suddenly Buddy threw a paper airplane at the teacher's back. It sailed right on past her and hit Donny Kale in the back of the head.

Mrs. Rudd turned abruptly and frowned. "All right—who threw it?"

The room grew silent and still.

Mrs. Rudd kept looking around. "We'll just sit quietly and wait until we find out who did this. If we don't get the math done, you'll just have to take it home and finish it."

J. B. sneakily reached into his desk for his math book. *Crinkle crinkle crinkle tic tic tic.* J. B. froze. Without even looking he knew paper airplanes fell out of *his* desk.

Mrs. Rudd raised her eyebrows. "You, J. B.?" She continued on to her desk. "I'm surprised."

"But I—"

She waved her hand to cut him off. "You'll spend today's recesses cleaning out the supply closet."

J. B. glared at Buddy, who looked serious. Only his eyes gave him away. Inside, Buddy was probably laughing his head off.

The rest of the day didn't get any better. When Mrs. Rudd returned last week's spelling tests, Emory had a *B*, and J. B. a *C +*. Of course, Buddy got an *A*.

Buddy shook his head and clicked his tongue. "Shame, shame, Wigglebottom."

J. B. kicked the rung of Buddy's chair. "Be quiet and turn around, would you?"

In the afternoon when Mrs. Rudd paired them up for square dancing, J. B. scowled along with the other boys. He bowed halfheartedly to Sharilee Peters when the record started. Over and over the caller sang commands: "Promenade." "Do si do." "Allemande left." "Allemande right." Then, as J. B. checked the clock for what seemed like the ten-thousandth time, the dismissal bell finally rang.

J. B. went to his desk and gathered his things. Emory waited by the door for him, and they walked out together.

J. B. picked up a stick and dragged it along beside him. "Are you mad at me for calling you Einstein at the field yesterday?"

Emory shrugged. "Not really, I guess. But I like it better when you say it as a compliment." They walked for a while in silence.

"I hate the way Buddy acts," J. B. finally blurted out. "He's been treating me crummy ever since first grade when my dad was the 'room mother.'" J. B. shuddered. "That year his teasing was awful. Why can't he just leave me alone?"

"If you pretended like he didn't bother you, he'd probably leave you alone."

"But he *does* bother me!"

As they neared his house, J. B. noticed Bailey's rope lying in the grass. He quickly searched the yard with his eyes, but he didn't see the dog anywhere. J. B. threw one arm into the air. "I don't believe it."

Emory stopped and looked at him funny.

"You sure have been acting weird lately. You okay?"

J. B. sprinted off toward his backyard. "That all depends on whether Bailey ate my toast and jam!" he yelled over his shoulder.

Chapter 7

J. B. slid to a stop under the trees. "All right!"

In the dirt, where he had left it earlier, lay the toast and jam. And it was swarming with black ants.

He dropped his backpack in the dirt and ran to his room for the peanut can. He was glad Emory didn't stop. If he explained his plan to him, Emory would come up with some scientific reason why it probably wouldn't work.

A minute later he was back outside. With a small twig, J. B. scraped the ants off the toast and into the can. Some of the ants tried to crawl up the twig toward his hand, but J. B. gently shook them off. Before going inside, he put the toast back underneath the trees. He was sure there was still enough jam to attract more ants.

"Your snack is ready," Mom called from the window.

In all the excitement, J. B. had forgotten about his after-school snack. He squinted while he thought. Thursday. That meant carrot circles and celery logs for a snack. He wrinkled his nose. Thursday also meant meat loaf for dinner. Mmmm. The thought of meat loaf made his mouth get all juicy.

He looked in the kitchen doorway. Mom sat at the table sewing flowers onto the bottom of one of Kate's dresses. She sipped tea from her favorite mug.

"I don't want a snack today, Mom." J. B. headed down the hall.

Mom put down her sewing and followed him. "Do you feel all right, honey?"

That name again! Yuk! "Fine, Mom. I just have a lot of homework."

She hesitated outside his door. J. B. didn't like the funny look on her face. He smiled. "You'll see. I'll eat twice as much meat loaf tonight as I usually do."

"If you're sure . . ."

"I'm sure, Mom. Give my snack to Kate." He closed his door.

Gently, he tapped the peanut can on his dresser. When he thought all the ants were at the bottom of the can, J. B. lifted the lid a crack. He peeked in. Yep, he thought, smiling. One more toast full of ants and he would have plenty.

He closed the lid, then wondered if the ants needed to breathe. Any air holes would have to be small enough so the ants couldn't escape. J. B. drummed his fingers on his dresser. He could ask to borrow one of Mom's sewing pins, but then she'd ask questions.

He yanked open his junk drawer and fished around. Finally, he found a KEEP SMILING button and used the pin on back to poke five tiny holes in the plastic lid.

J. B. dropped the button back in his drawer and glanced around his room. Now he needed a board.

He hurried to the garage and flicked on the light. A wagon, a sled, four bikes, his dad's tools, a broken TV, the lawn mower, and the freezer. Where would he find a board?

Finally he spotted some boards on the shelf under Dad's workbench. He held them up, one at a time, until he found one just the right size. Then he carried it back to his room.

J. B. lightly penciled *Buddy is a creep* on one side of the board. He held up the board and imagined how it would look tomorrow. He grinned. Then, remembering how he felt every time Buddy made fun of him, J. B. sighed and turned the board over. Anyway, the teachers and Mr. Westin wouldn't like it either. And they were the ones voting.

J. B. neatly penciled *J. B. Higgenbottom* on the back side of the board and leaned it against his wall. That's all he could do for now. His idea just had to work!

Someone knocked softly on his door.

"Come in."

Kate pushed open the door. "Hi, J. B." She held out her hand. "Want a carrot circle?"

He shook his head. "No thanks."

She held out her other hand. "I saved a jelly bean for you. Don't tell Mom, though. I snuck them from the cupboard."

J. B. smiled and took the piece of candy. This

was one of those times he liked having Kate for a little sister. He felt close to her, maybe because she shared a secret with him, just like friends do. "Kate, I'm really sorry for being so grouchy to you yesterday. I, well . . ." He thought about explaining to her how tough life gets when you're ten, but then changed his mind.

"That's okay." She jumped up on his bed. "I learned to read five more words in school today. Want to hear them?"

"Sure." He sat down next to her.

"In." Kate held up one finger. "Out." She held up another finger. "Go." She held up a third finger, then shoved the last carrot circle in her mouth and stared at the ceiling for a moment. "I can't remember the other two." She played with a button on her shirt. "I learned another word too, but I can't say it. It's a bad word that Carl wrote in the dirt at recess. Then he got sent in."

J. B. tried not to grin. "That's good, Kate." He patted her head. "You like reading, don't you?"

"Yep." She scooted off the bed. "Someday I'll read as good as you."

"Yep, you will."

Kate pointed at the board leaning against his wall. "What's that for?"

"The assembly tomorrow. You'll just have to wait and see."

She looked around his room for a while and asked silly questions, then put her arms around his waist and hugged him. "I love you, J. B."

J. B. hugged her back. "I love you too."

She started to leave, then stopped in the doorway and turned around. "I almost forgot. Emory's on the phone."

"Now?"

"Yep. That's why I came to get you."

"But that was ten minutes ago, Kate!" He brushed past her and hurried to the phone. "Hello?" The line was dead. J. B. clicked the button, then dialed Emory's number. After ten rings, he hung up and stomped his foot.

"Mom! Mo-o-om!"

Mom peered around the kitchen doorway.

J. B. crossed his arms over his chest. "Kate answered the phone and didn't tell me until over ten minutes later it was for me. It was Emory, and he hung up. Now he's not home."

"Oh, J. B., don't be such a tattletale. He'll call back if it's important." Mom disappeared into the kitchen.

J. B. scowled. Don't be a tattletale! Kate tattled on him all the time and got him into trouble. "R-r-r-r—sisters!"

J. B. stomped to the hall closet. Maybe Mom was right; maybe the call wasn't important. Maybe Emory just wanted him to go to the ball field. He pulled his math book out of his backpack. No way was he going to the field and chance running into Buddy. He'd had enough of him for one day.

It wasn't until after dinner that J. B. got to collect the last of his ants. "Perfect," he whispered, scraping them into his can.

He finished his homework and put on his pajamas, then flopped down on his bed and stared into the darkness. J. B. thought about the Parade of Pets and smiled. Finally he fell asleep and dreamed.

Chapter 8

It was a terrific dream.

The gymnasium bleachers were packed with kids. It was J. B.'s turn in the Parade of Pets. His ants rode out on the back of a two-headed zebra. The ants bowed to each other, then promenaded to the square-dance caller's command. Even the band was made up of ants playing tiny instruments.

The crowd in the gym cheered as the ants danced. J. B. smiled and waved to them. The crowd clapped.

Then it was Buddy's turn to show his pet.

Buddy pulled something from his pocket and cupped it in his hand.

The kids in the bleachers grew silent.

J. B.'s heart pounded. He struggled to see. Suddenly he caught sight of what Buddy held in his hand and burst into laughter. It was a family of fleas he'd taken off Bailey.

"Boo! Hiss!" The kids in the bleachers pelted Buddy with spit wads.

The president of the United States stood up from his seat in the bleachers.

The crowd quieted.

The president cleared his throat. "The winner is . . ." He paused. "The winner is J. B. Wigglebottom!"

"Higgenbottom!" J. B. shouted as the crowd broke into a roar. Kids poured out of the bleachers at him, then two boys hoisted him up onto their shoulders. "J. B.!" everyone shouted. "J. B.!"

High above the cheering crowd, J. B. waved. People were everywhere, as far as he could see. Why, he could even see his mother.

His mother! J. B.'s eyelids blinked, then flew open. He was in bed!

Mom poked at his shoulder. "Are you awake

yet? I've been standing here calling your name over and over. Your pancakes are getting cold."

Pancakes. That meant today was Friday. He'd only dreamed about the Parade of Pets.

"I'm awake!" J. B. jumped out of bed and threw on his clothes. He couldn't be late for school today.

After breakfast J. B. put on his backpack and gathered his lunch, his board, and his can into his arms.

"Ready to go, J. B.?" Kate asked.

"Yep. Come on, let's go."

Kate opened the door for him, then followed him out with Bimbo. "What's all that stuff for?"

"The Parade of Pets." He grinned. "You'll see." J. B. headed toward school. He looked for Emory, but didn't see him. He was glad it was a cool day for his ants.

Kate looked at the picture on the can. "Peanuts? Are you bringing an elephant to the parade?"

J. B. laughed. "Nope. I-I-I—" He froze. "I forgot the strawberry jam!"

"What?" Kate looked at him blankly.

"Never mind, just go on to school." He clutched his stuff tighter and raced back to the house.

His mom looked up from the picture she was sewing with black knots. "What are you doing home?"

He put his stuff down, opened the refrigerator, and pushed the food around. "I need the strawberry jam." He glanced up and saw the funny look on Mom's face. "It's for a school project."

"Sorry, honey, it's all gone. You used the last of it yesterday."

J. B. swallowed hard. Without the jam, his ants were useless. His knees began to shake and his arms went limp. Buddy would never let him hear the end of this.

Mom put her hand to J. B.'s forehead. "You're as white as the refrigerator. Are you feeling all right, honey?"

Honey? Honey! What a great idea! If ants liked sweet, sticky strawberry jam, then they should also like sweet, sticky honey. And his mom had creamed honey for her tea.

J. B. brightened. "I'm fine, Mom, fine. Can I use your honey for my project?"

"I suppose, but—"

"Thanks, Mom." He hugged her, then grabbed the honey from the cupboard. He picked up his backpack, lunch, board, and can, then ran back to school.

He carefully sidestepped Buddy's outstretched foot, set his stuff on his desk, and slid into his seat. He reached his hand in and checked his desk for paper airplanes, or something worse.

Buddy grinned. "Made your sister carry your pet to school, huh, Wigglebottom? A stuffed monkey, right?"

J. B. smiled and pulled his ant can out of Buddy's reach. "No, Buddy. That's Kate's show-and-tell. I have something great this year."

Emory looked surprised; Buddy's grin melted away.

J. B. sat up taller. He wanted to jump for joy.

A second later he froze. Maybe he shouldn't have said anything. Maybe his idea wasn't neat. Maybe ants didn't like honey. Maybe—

The morning bell rang.

Chapter 9

J.B. looked around the room while Mrs. Rudd took a silent roll call. Boxes sat on a lot of the desks. Most were shoe boxes with holes poked in the lids. Emory had a bigger box. Kelly-Lynn Daniels had an even bigger box. Mindy Adams had something covered with a white cloth on her desk. Probably a bird. Rhett Miller and Buddy didn't have anything on top of their desks.

J. B. sucked on his tongue. Did he really have a chance at winning? Maybe Buddy didn't bring a pet to the parade. Or maybe he brought one of everything from his dad's store and they were all stashed in the supply closet. J. B. was so nervous it was hard to sit still.

Mrs. Rudd stood up. "Okay, class, *quietly* line up in alphabetical order."

They all carried their pets over to the door and found their places.

"Are any parents here to help?" Mrs. Rudd asked.

Rhett Miller and Buddy raised their hands. "My mom's waiting outside," Rhett said.

"My dad's in the parking lot," Buddy said.

Mrs. Rudd motioned them out the door, then pointed down the walkway. "Meet us at that gymnasium door. We'll go in there."

Rhett nodded. Buddy shook his head. "I think it's better if my dad keeps the r—" He clamped his lips together for a second. "I think my pet should stay outside until it's my turn."

J. B. rolled his eyes. Buddy always had to make a big deal over his own stuff. What a show-off.

"Okay, Buddy." Mrs. Rudd led the class down the hall and outside. At the gym door she held up her hand. The class stopped. When everyone was silent and still, Mrs. Rudd opened the door and peeked in. She looked back at the line. "The other students are already seated in the west bleachers. There's a microphone up front for us to use." She ran her hand along the wall. "Once inside the gym, we will line up against this wall. Please wait *quietly* until it's your turn. Any questions?"

No one raised a hand.

"Okay then, let's go. Don't forget, if your pet knows a trick, have him do it while you're at the microphone. Once you leave the front of the room, you don't get to go back."

They filed inside. J. B.'s heart beat faster. He should've tried his trick once to see if it would really work.

He looked into the bleachers. The older kids were in the top rows. In the very bottom row he spotted Kate. She held Bimbo with one hand and waved to J. B. with the other. Then she sneezed. She sneezed again and again and again. When she stopped, she rubbed her eyes and looked at J. B.

He waved back to her. Poor Kate. It must be awful to have allergies.

Mindy Adams walked up to the microphone and pulled the cloth off her cage. J. B. had been right. It was a bird cage.

"This is Mickey, my parakeet," Mindy said. She held the cage closer to the microphone. "Say hello, Mickey."

"Hello, Mickey; hello, Mickey."

All the kids laughed. Mindy smiled and covered her cage. Everyone clapped, then Mrs. Rudd pointed for Mindy to line up again at the wall.

J. B. shifted his weight from one foot to the other foot. He had to admit, a talking bird was pretty neat, even if it didn't sing "Yankee Doodle."

Next there were white mice. A goldfish in a plastic bowl was after that, then a stuffed kangaroo with a secret hiding place. He could tell by the low, dull clap no one liked the kangaroo much. Kelly-Lynn Daniels showed a pure white cat with four black-and-white kittens. The mother cat only had three legs, but she could still run. And she used a leash, just like a dog.

J. B. crossed his fingers. So far Mindy's bird and the three-legged cat were the only pets that did anything neat.

Suddenly J. B. felt weak. He put his stuff on the floor and hurried over to Mrs. Rudd.

"Yes, J. B.?"

"May I go back to the classroom? I need to get something else for my trick."

"Yes, J. B., but hurry. It's almost your turn."

J. B. took quiet giant steps out of the gym, then raced back to the room. He scanned the room again and again. A few seconds later he grabbed two erasers and ran back to the gym.

Emory stood at the microphone. He held a metal cage up high. Tinker huddled inside. "She doesn't know any tricks, but she's soft and cuddly," Emory said. "And she doesn't bite. I like to hold her." He started to walk away, then leaned back toward the microphone. "Oh. And I don't have to take her outside to go to the bathroom."

The kids laughed, even though J. B. knew Emory didn't mean it to be funny. J. B. felt bad for Emory, but Emory seemed unbothered by it all. He smiled and put Tinker's cage back into the box.

Suddenly J. B.'s heart pounded, loud and hard, in his chest and his ears. It was time to show his ants!

Chapter 10

With each step he took toward the bleachers, J. B.'s knees wobbled a little more. Finally he reached the microphone. He was sure his voice would be as shaky as his legs.

"It—" A shrill whistle from the loudspeakers made J. B. jump back from the microphone. Some of the kids covered their ears; some of them made noises. J. B. stepped back up to the microphone, but not quite so close.

"It will take me a few minutes to get things ready." He wondered if the microphone picked up the pounding of his heart. No one laughed, so he guessed it didn't.

J. B. kneeled, put one eraser on the floor and

stacked the other one on top. He held the board in one hand, then dipped one finger of his other hand into the honey. As he was about to use the honey to trace over his name on the board, he heard Kate talking to another kid. "That's my brother, J. B. He's really smart. His pet will be better than anyone's."

"What is it?" the kid asked.

"I don't know," Kate said. "But it'll be good."

Listening to Kate made J. B. feel warm inside. He began to relax. Kate was a pretty good little sister—most of the time. He glanced up at her. She was even kind of cute.

Ignoring the letters he'd printed on the board, J. B. used the honey to write three new words. Then he propped the board up against the erasers.

J. B. was about to remove the lid from his peanut can when he noticed Mrs. Rudd's feet next to his board. He looked up.

"Where's your box, J. B.?"

"Box?"

"For your pet. You need a box or a leash. Do you have one of those?"

A box! His heart began to pound again. He

had forgotten a box! And as soon as he opened the lid the ants might run all over the place.

J. B. set down his can, then leaned into the microphone. "Just a second." The audience stirred. He ran over to Emory. "I forgot a box. Can I borrow yours?"

At the end of the line, Buddy snickered. J. B. answered him with a glare.

Emory took off the lid and removed Tinker's cage. He handed the box to J. B. "Good luck."

"Thanks, Emory. I knew I could count on you." He hurried back to the microphone.

J. B. kneeled behind the box. He stacked the erasers inside, then set the bottom edge of the board on the erasers. He leaned the back of the board against the back side of the box, at a perfect angle for the kids to see.

After gently tapping the peanut can on the floor, J. B. removed the lid. Starting at the top left edge, he poured the ants onto the board. His hands shook. Would his idea really work?

Whispers floated through the air.

The first two letters J. B. had written in honey, the K and A, were now black with ants. It was working!

Some kids in the first row oohed and aahed.

J. B. looked up. Someone else squealed. "Wow!" Someone shouted from the audience.

J. B. held his breath and looked at his board. In thick black letters the ants spelled out

KATE IS GR

His idea was working!

The crowd wiggled and whispered. J. B. let out his breath and smiled at them. There were more oohs and aahs. They loved him!

A moment later the crowd hushed. Something was wrong.

J. B. looked down at his board. He was running out of ants!

Oh no, oh no, oh no, oh no, oh no. What could he do? And now it felt as if his heart were about to explode in his head.

J. B. blinked and looked closer. Some of the ants were down in the bottom of the box. Gently, with his finger, he nudged them toward the last three letters.

The ants crawled up to the honey. The last

three letters were thin, but at least they could be seen.

"Kate is great," someone read out loud.

"Hey, that's pretty neat," Rhett Miller said.

Kate squealed. "That's me!" She stood up and jumped up and down. "And that's my brother, J. B.!" Her smile was the brightest J. B. had ever seen. He felt good inside and out. A little bit embarrassed too; he felt his face get hot. He gathered his stuff and headed toward the wall.

Buddy passed him on his way outside. His grin was so big J. B. could see his back teeth. He slapped J. B. on the back. "Not bad, Wigglebottom. But wait'll you see mine."

Chapter 11

J. B. kneeled behind Emory, opened the peanut can, and tried to slide the ants in. The harder he tried, the faster they headed for the patches of honey.

He looked at the metal handle sticking out of Emory's pocket. "Pssst!" he whispered. "Can I borrow your spoon?"

Emory nodded, took the spoon from his back pocket, and handed it to J. B.

J. B. put a little blob of honey in the bottom of his can, then used the spoon to scrape and carry the ants. Occasionally he'd glance up to check out the pets.

A few of his ants jumped or fell to the floor,

but J. B. stuck his hand down to stop them from escaping. When he was done, he used his shirt to wipe the honey off the spoon, then handed the spoon and box back to Emory.

Emory stuffed the spoon back in his pocket, but didn't take the box. "Use it to carry your stuff."

"Thanks." J. B. shifted from one foot to the other as he watched the different animals being showed. Mostly he thought about Buddy.

Rhett Miller, with help from his mom, brought in his dog. It was a big Irish setter named Cinnamon. He could stand on two legs. He could shake hands too. Neat tricks, J. B. thought, but not *great* tricks. He hoped the teachers thought so too.

There were a lot more cats in the parade, one bunny, and three hamsters.

When Jenny Stanley pulled out her snake, some of the girls screamed. The snake couldn't do any tricks, but J. B. thought Jenny was neat because she wasn't afraid to hold a snake.

Finally it was Buddy's turn. J. B. took a deep breath and held it in for a few seconds.

Mr. Zimmers, Buddy's dad, helped him pull out a big cage on wheels. Covering the cage was a bright pink sheet that had huge yellow flowers on it. J. B. hoped the kids would laugh at Buddy's weird sheet. They didn't. They all sat very still and waited for Buddy to unveil the cage.

Buddy watched his father walk back to the doorway. Then, when all eyes were on him, Buddy yanked the sheet off the cage.

Everyone oohed. J. B.'s heart pounded wildly. This was the best animal Buddy had ever brought to the parade.

"A baby ostrich!" someone cried.

Buddy sneered, held up his hands, and waited for it to get quiet again. "This is *not* a baby ostrich," he said into the microphone. "It might look like a baby ostrich to *you*. Actually, it's a rhea and he's almost full grown. His name is Ace."

The crowd whispered to each other. A knot formed in J. B.'s stomach. He could tell that the kids really liked the rhea. That meant the teachers and Mr. Westin would like it too.

A boy from the kindergarten section waved his hand wildly in the air. "Is he really your pet?"

Buddy shook his head. "Naw. My dad is transporting him to a wildlife park where he'll have lots of room to run."

The boy scowled. "Can he do any tricks?"

J. B. crossed his fingers.

Buddy began to fidget. "He's a great swimmer, but I couldn't bring a swimming pool to school." Buddy laughed. Nobody else laughed.

J. B. brightened. Maybe he had a chance of winning after all. Just then Buddy glanced his way and saw him smiling. He glared at J. B. and stepped closer to the cage.

"There is one trick Ace can do," Buddy said. "When he runs he can change his direction really fast. All he does is raise and lower his wings, just like a pilot does with airplane rudders. That's why he's called Ace."

J. B. uncrossed his fingers. Buddy *couldn't* show that trick as long as Ace was locked in a cage.

Buddy looked directly at J. B. A show-all-your-teeth grin spread across his face. "Watch this!" And he threw open the cage door.

"Buddy, no!" Mr. Zimmers yelled. But it was too late.

Ace scrambled out of his cage and zigzagged across the gym. A roar went up from the crowd.

Ace ran back and forth in front of the bleachers, trying to find a way out. Some of the little kids in the front row squealed and jumped up into the next row. Soon, most of the kids were laughing.

Mr. Westin ran back and forth, back and forth. "My floor! My floor! He's scratching my floor!"

J. B. looked down when Ace ran by him. The rhea had three big toes on each foot. With each giant step he took, he scratched the floor.

Ace ran around and around. Buddy chased him. Mr. Zimmers ran after them both. Mr. Westin kept waving his hands and shouting, "My floor! My floor!"

Poor Ace! He looked so frightened J. B. was sure his heart was pounding in his chest *and* his ears.

75

Chapter

12

Panting, Buddy gave up the chase and fell in line with his class. He slid down the wall and plopped on the floor. He looked as if he were going to throw up.

Mr. Zimmers grabbed the flowered sheet and continued chasing Ace.

J. B. was enjoying the sight of Ace turning corners. It reminded him of when he was little, how he used to stick out his arms and go zooming around the living room like an airplane. Once, he'd accidentally knocked over a glass owl and chipped it. "Oh, J. B.," Dad had said calmly, "airplanes fly outside in wide, open spaces, not inside."

J. B. thought a rhea should probably be outside too.

Mr. Zimmers tossed the sheet at Ace. He missed. He threw the sheet again and again. The kids laughed and squealed. "Run, Ace, run!" someone shouted.

Finally Mr. Westin quit yelling about the floor. He stuck out his arms and blocked Ace's way, just like a guard in a basketball game. Then, with the help of the janitor, Mr. Zimmers threw the sheet over Ace.

Ace pecked at them through the sheet. He kicked at them too. Mr. Zimmers stood firm. "Darn you, hold still!" Soon Mr. Zimmers, Mr. Westin, and the janitor maneuvered Ace back into his cage.

Suddenly J. B. remembered Kate. His eyes searched the bleachers. Was she okay? Finally he spotted her. She was trying, in between sneezes, to talk to another girl.

When everyone settled down, Mrs. Rudd led her class to the gym door. All except Buddy. His father pulled him from the line. They stood in the corner talking. Mostly, Mr. Zimmers talked, and Buddy listened: ". . . upsetting . . . poor animal . . . authorities . . ."

Mr. Zimmers pointed his finger too, jerking it up and down to emphasize his words.

As his class filed out, J. B. stole one last look at Buddy. His face was very, very red, and J. B. couldn't tell for sure, but from the way Buddy was rubbing his eyes, he might have been crying.

J. B. wondered if his own dad would've gotten that mad if J. B. had done the same thing. Maybe. Maybe not. Just *thinking* about it caused J. B.'s heart to thump.

Back in the classroom, when they were all seated, Emory held Tinker's cage up to his face and whispered to her. Everyone seemed to be whispering.

J. B. tried to listen to what was being said about the parade, but it was hard trying to listen to everyone talk at once. They all seemed to really like Mindy's bird; even now he was getting a lot of attention. Someone said something about his ants too. He couldn't hear if it was good or bad. Mostly, everyone talked about the rhea. It was definitely unforgettable.

Emory put Tinker's cage down and leaned forward. "Where'd you get such a neat idea for the ants?"

J. B. shrugged. "From the cupcakes, I guess. Did you really like it?"

Emory nodded. "I hope you win."

"Thanks." He felt lucky to have Emory for his best friend. "Can you play after school? I'll bring your box back."

"I don't need the box, J. B., but come over anyway."

J. B. nodded, thought for a second, then cocked his head. "How come you don't want to win?"

Emory leaned his chin on Tinker's cage and raised his eyebrows. "I got a red ribbon in the City Science Fair." He grinned and pulled out his spoon. "Know what else I can do with this?"

J. B. shook his head. "Scrape ants into a peanut can?"

Emory scooted closer. "No-o-o. This spoon can hold more liquid than you think." He held the spoon up to eye level. "If you fill it with water, the volume you can get *in* the spoon is actually larger than the *apparent* volume *of* the spoon. Water can stand above the rim." He smiled. "Like magic!" He put away the spoon. "Actually, it's the surface tension of the water that lets you overfill it. It has nothing to do with the spoon." He leaned back in his chair. "Neat, huh?"

"Really neat, Emory." J. B. turned back around. Even though he didn't always understand right away what Emory was saying, he knew it would turn out to be something amazing.

Mrs. Rudd stood up from her desk and waited for the class to get quiet. Finally she cleared her throat. "I'm very proud of how you behaved in the gym. For the most part, that was a terrific parade." She leaned against her desk and sighed. "It was great seeing all the different kinds of animals."

She grabbed some dittos from her desk and passed them out. "Now it's time to put your pets away and do some work. You can *quietly* work these math problems while I go to Mr. Westin's office to vote."

The door squeaked open. Everyone stared as Buddy stepped inside. He turned the color of raw hamburger.

Mrs. Rudd raised an eyebrow, then handed him a ditto. "I certainly know which animal was most exciting," she said.

Everyone laughed. Everyone except J. B.

Buddy straightened up and strutted to his desk, stomping on J. B.'s foot as he slid into his seat.

A lump formed in J. B.'s throat. He thought about his ants, then he thought about Ace. He swallowed hard. If being the *most exciting* made you the most unforgettable, he was dead. There was no way he could win the Parade of Pets.

Chapter 13

Sure that he wouldn't be the winner of the parade, J. B. found it hard to keep his mind on his math. Every time he looked at Buddy, Buddy gave him that big, toothy smile.

J. B. shifted in his chair. If he couldn't be the winner of the Parade of Pets, he hoped Mindy could. Or Rhett. Or one of the other kids. Anyone but Buddy. J. B. couldn't take another year of Buddy teasing him.

He pressed too hard while carrying in a multiplication problem and broke his pencil lead. After checking to make sure his shoes hadn't been tied together, he rose and went to the pencil sharpener. *R-r-r-r-r-r. R-r-r-r-r-r.*

When the point was sharp, he blew off the dust and returned to his seat. A piece of candy lay on top of his math paper. J. B. fingered it. *Fancy Chocolate* he read from the wrapper. *Imported from Switzerland.*

"My dad brought them at Kmart," Emory leaned forward and whispered in a breath of chocolate.

"Thanks," J. B. said. But even the thought of fancy candy didn't make him feel better. J. B. slipped the chocolate into his pocket, then continued with his assignment.

Ten minutes before the dismissal bell rang, Mr. Westin walked into the classroom. He held a small piece of paper in one hand. He leaned close and whispered something to Mrs. Rudd.

Mrs. Rudd smiled. "Mr. Westin is going to announce the winner now, class."

It sounded as if everyone sucked in his or her breath at the same time. J. B. rested one elbow on his desk and set his chin in his hand.

"I'm proud of this year's winner," Mr. Westin said.

Buddy sat up very straight and tall, turned, and grinned at J. B.

"This year's winner brought a most interesting pet," Mr. Westin said. "Actually *pet* isn't the correct word here, but you know we take all kinds of entries into the parade, including stuffed ones."

For a second J. B. thought the kangaroo had won. But that was too hard to believe. Then he remembered the little kid asking Buddy if Ace was his *pet.* *"Naw,"* Buddy had replied. J. B. sagged. Buddy had won again.

Mr. Westin glanced at his paper. "Oh, yes, there is an extra surprise for the winner this year. On Monday, he *or* she will also get their picture taken. That picture will go into the newspaper with a story about him."

Everyone made some sort of oohing sound and wiggled in their seats. Everyone, except Buddy.

Mr. Westin held his hands in front of him, tapped his left fingers against his right fingers, and paced. "I'd like to mention that since the parade started eight years ago, never has one pet received so many votes as this year's winner."

Everyone oohed again.

"Maybe it's because it was presented in such an original fashion," Mr. Westin said.

Buddy was still grinning and now he was starting to wiggle too.

J. B. looked at the clock. Two minutes until the final bell. He didn't know which was worse, listening to Mr. Westin right now telling everyone how great Buddy is, or, in a few minutes, listening to Buddy himself telling everyone how great he is.

Mr. Westin cleared his throat and spoke louder. "It gives me great pleasure to announce to you the winner of this year's Parade of Pets. Congratulations, Jonathon Bradford Higgenbottom!"

J. B.'s chin slipped off his hand. *He won!* His heart raced. It pounded in his chest and his ears. *He won!*

Emory slapped him on the back. "That's great, J. B."

The other kids swarmed around and slapped him on the back too. "Yea, Wigglebottom!" "Way to go, J. B.!" "Good going, Higgenbottom!"

Mr. Westin came over and shook his hand. "Very creative, Jonathon. I'm looking forward to our lunch on Monday."

"Thanks."

J. B. nudged Buddy in the back. He was going to smile his biggest smile at him, but he noticed Buddy's eyes were watery. J. B. quickly looked away. He didn't want Buddy to cry. Until now, he'd thought Buddy was too mean to feel bad about anything.

J. B. turned toward Emory, but Emory was staring off into space. He had the same look he'd had Wednesday at the ball field when he didn't stick up for J. B.

J. B. waved his hand in front of Emory's face. "Hello-o-o, Emory."

Emory blinked. "Sorry. I was thinking about my spoon again."

Maybe that's why Emory hadn't defended him at the field. Maybe he hadn't been listening!

The final bell rang.

J. B. stuffed his math ditto into his backpack and headed down the aisle with the other kids.

At the door, Mrs. Rudd stopped him. "Congratulations, J. B. Such a unique idea. Remember to wear something nice for your picture Monday."

J. B. smiled. "I will. Thanks." When he stepped outside Buddy tried to trip him, then ran off. J. B.'s anger flared, then died.

Emory slugged his arm as they headed home. "It'll be great getting your picture in the paper."

"Yeah." J. B.'s steps were light and bouncy. He looked down at the box in his arms. "I'll tell them I got the box from you." He was so glad he had Emory for a friend.

The boys stopped in front of J. B.'s house. Kate waved to them from the window.

"Come over right away," Emory said. "We'll celebrate. I'll even look for something to eat that's not health food. Something my mom didn't make."

J. B. looked to the window. "First, I want to talk to Kate and have her show me her sunflowers." Maybe he'd even tell her that he used to get away with murder too, when he was little. He smiled to himself. Naw. Maybe he wouldn't tell her that.

J. B. thought about the parade, about how

his ants turned out to be better than an exotic bird. His idea had actually worked. "You know, Emory, I don't think Buddy's teasing will bother me so much anymore."

"That's good." Emory hung his spoon on his nose, handle down. It stuck.

J. B. wondered if it stuck because of the honey, or if it was some sort of scientific trick. He ran across the yard and back to the tree camp. Kneeling, J. B. removed the lid from the peanut can. As the ants started to scatter, J. B. pulled the imported candy from his pocket and unwrapped it.

He'd never had candy from Switzerland before, at least not that he knew of. He held it close to his nose. It *smelled* special.

J. B. took one small bite and let the chocolate melt on his tongue. It *tasted* special. He nibbled off another bite. Smiling, J. B. set the candy down for the ants. "Thanks, guys. Happy celebrating."

Then J. B. stood up and went into the house to look for Kate.